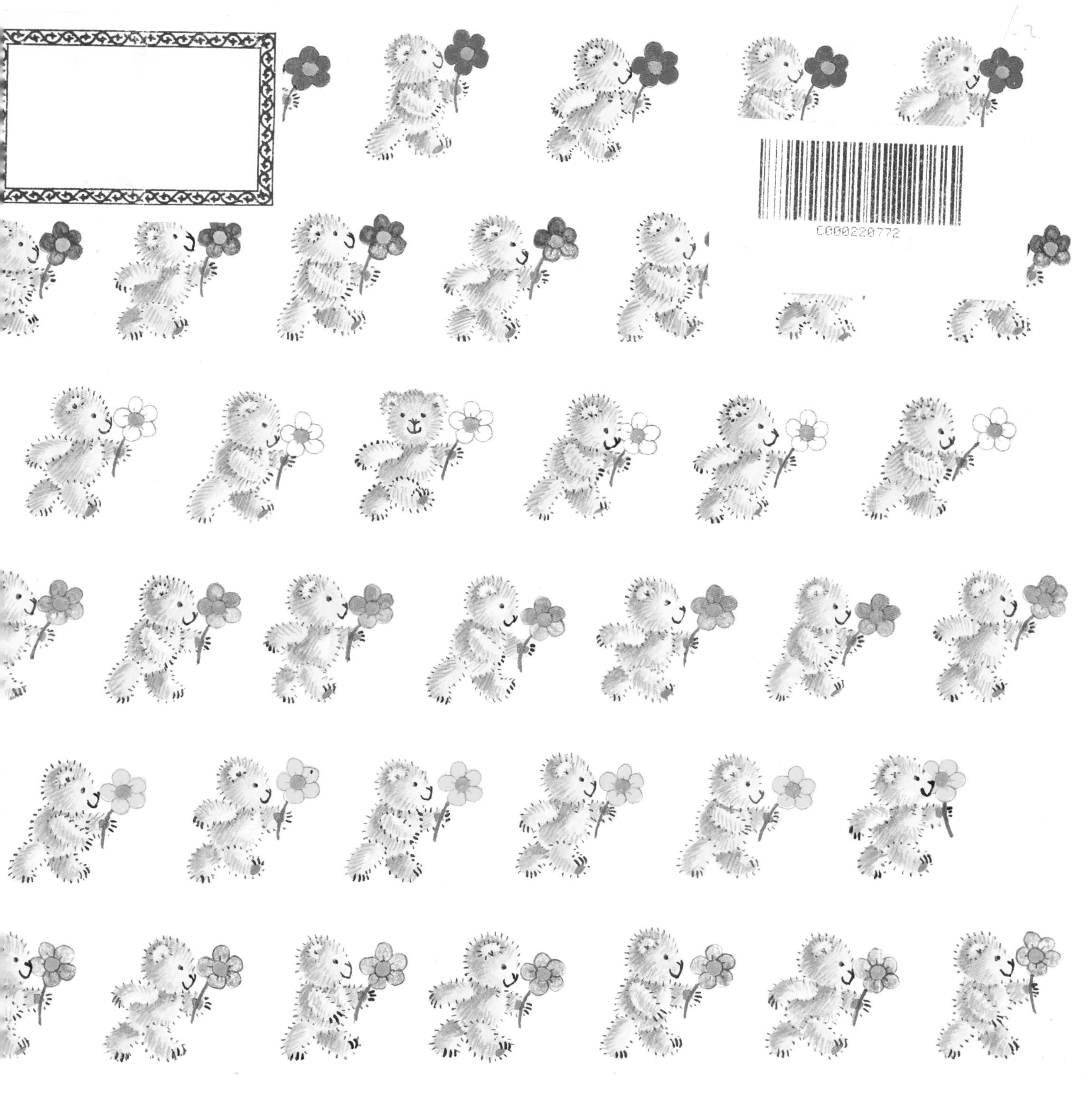
C000220772

Laura Downton

Teddy in the Garden

AMANDA DAVIDSON

COLLINS

For my nephews
Anthony and Ian

William Collins Sons & Co Ltd
London · Glasgow · Sydney · Auckland
Toronto · Johannesburg

First published 1986

ISBN 0 00 195824 0

Printed and bound in Belgium
by Henri Proost & CIE PVBA

Teddy is in the garden,

with all his friends.

He is wearing his favourite hat.

“Hey! That’s mine!” says Teddy.

"Give it back!"

"You naughty dog!" he cries.

Teddy chases after her.

And so do his friends.

"Oh, no! She's buried it!"

"We'll never find it now!" sighs Teddy.

They start to dig,

and find all sorts of things!

“What’s under here?” says Teddy.

"Hurray! My hat! I've found it!"

"Oh dear! It's moving!"

“Why it’s a . . .”

“Hedgehog!” says Teddy. “Hello.”

"Can I have my hat back, please?"

"Thank you. That's *much* better."

"Let's have tea."

“Peace at last,” smiles Teddy.

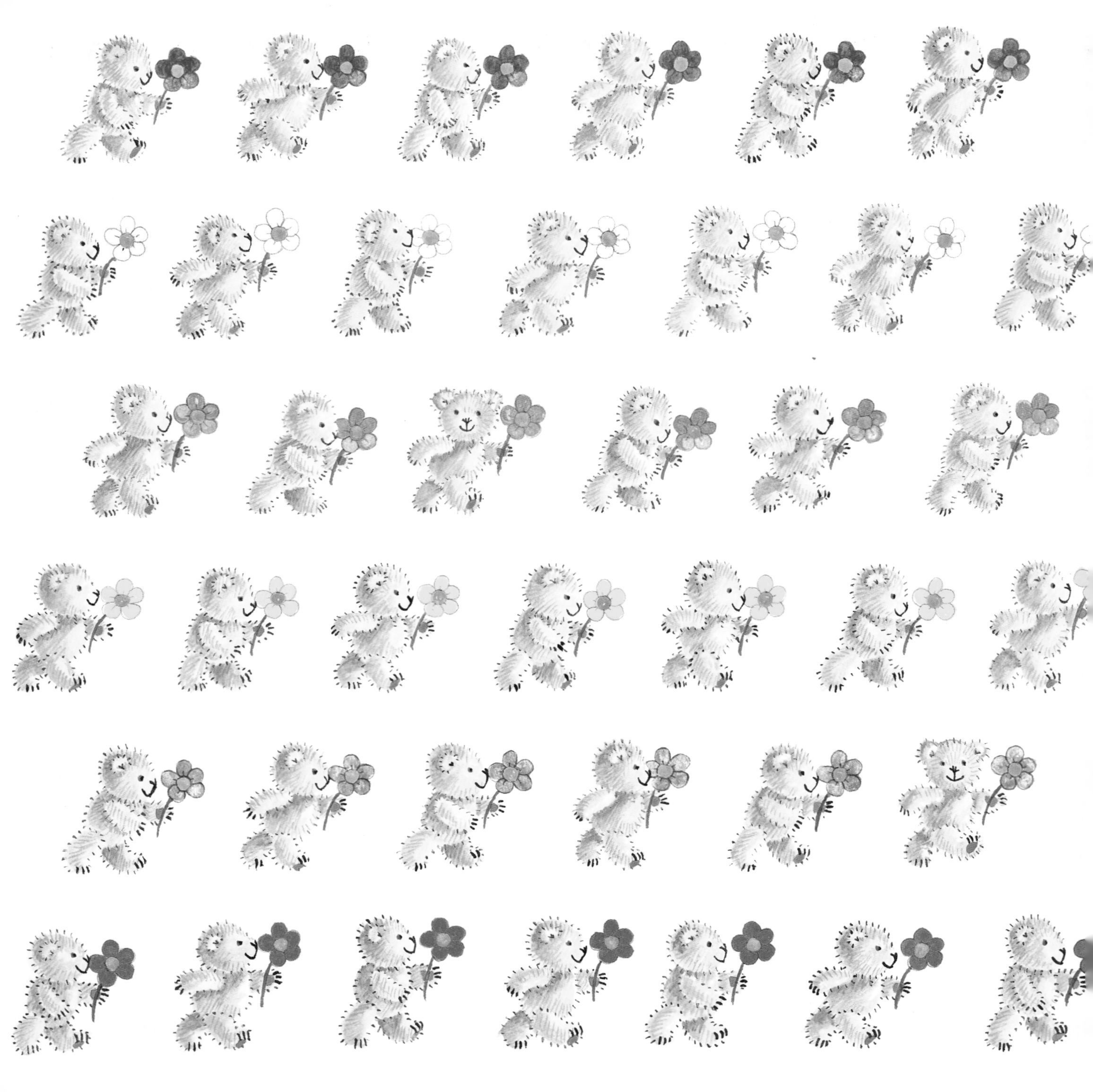